Around the World

Edited by Seth Rogers

Publishing Credits

Rachelle Cracchiolo, M.S.Ed., *Publisher*
Conni Medina, M.A.Ed., *Editor in Chief*
Nika Fabienke, Ed.D., *Content Director*
Véronique Bos, *Creative Director*
Shaun N. Bernadou, *Art Director*
Seth Rogers, *Editor*
Valerie Morales, *Associate Editor*
Kevin Pham, *Graphic Designer*

Library of Congress Cataloging-in-Publication Data

Names: Rogers, Seth, editor.
Title: Around the world / edited by Seth Rogers.
Description: Huntington Beach, CA : Teacher Created Materials, [2020] | Includes book club questions. | Audience: Age 13. | Audience: Grades 4-6. | Summary: "From eastern Europe to South America, people have been telling stories all over the world for centuries. This book has collected a few traditional short stories from around the world for you to enjoy!"-- Provided by publisher.
Identifiers: LCCN 2019031467 (print) | LCCN 2019031468 (ebook) | ISBN 9781644913505 (paperback) | ISBN 9781644914403 (ebook)
Subjects: LCSH: Readers (Elementary) | Tales.
Classification: LCC PE1119 .A6825 2020 (print) | LCC PE1119 (ebook) | DDC 428.6/2--dc23
LC record available at https://lccn.loc.gov/2019031467
LC ebook record available at https://lccn.loc.gov/2019031468

Image Credits

Illustrated by: Front cover, p.1, pp.9–14 Sebastian Baculea; pp.4–8 Estella Millbanks; pp.15–19 Biry Sarkis; pp.20–25 Juana Martinez Neal; pp.26–31 Juana Martinez Neal. Courtesy Luma Creative Limited. All rights reserved.

TCM | Teacher Created Materials

5301 Oceanus Drive
Huntington Beach, CA 92649-1030
www.tcmpub.com

ISBN 978-1-6449-1350-5

© 2020 Teacher Created Materials, Inc.
Printed in China
Nordica.082019.CA21901557

Table of Contents

Wolf Lullaby 4

The Frog and the Condor 9

The Tree of Dreams 15

The Language of Birds 20

Brer Rabbit 26

Book Club Questions 32

Wolf Lullaby

On a Caribbean island, there was once a sweet little house, surrounded by a sweet little garden with a sweet little picket fence around it. A sweet little girl lived there with her father.

Around the house was a pretty wildflower meadow, and beyond the meadow was the forest where the big, bad wolves lived. Every morning, the little girl's father would say to her, "You can play in the garden today, dear, but whatever you do, don't open the gate. Not far from our house is the big forest, and that's where the big, bad wolves live." And every day, the girl did exactly as she was told, because she was a good little girl. Except for one day.

On that day, she was singing a sweet little song to herself and picking a bouquet of flowers. "Traybla, traybla, cum qua, kimo. Traybla, traybla, cum qua, kimo," she sang. And as she sang, she saw in the meadow the most beautiful yellow flower she had ever seen.

Oh, that flower would look so nice in my bouquet, she thought. And as she gazed at it, its petals seemed to dance in the breeze.

She checked that her father wasn't watching, and she looked all around for wolves. When she was sure it was safe, she opened the gate and walked into the meadow, still singing, "Traybla, traybla, cum qua, kimo." She picked a yellow flower and put it in her hair.

She was about to turn around and head back to her garden when she saw another yellow flower a little further out in the meadow. It was even prettier than the first one.

How lovely! thought the little girl. She checked that her father wasn't watching, and she looked all around for wolves, then, still singing "Traybla, traybla, cum qua, kimo," she picked this yellow flower, too.

She was about to turn around and head back to her garden when she spotted a whole patch of pretty yellow flowers near the edge of the forest.

So, she checked that her father wasn't watching, she looked all around for wolves, and when she was sure it was safe, she walked over to the yellow flowers and picked them all, still singing, "Traybla, traybla, cum qua, kimo."

All this time, a hungry wolf had been spying on the girl from behind a tree, and just as she was about to head home, he sprang out in front of her.

When she saw the wolf's greedy eyes and sharp teeth, she shook with fear.

"What a sweet song that was, little girl. Sing it to me again," snapped the wolf, and he licked his lips.

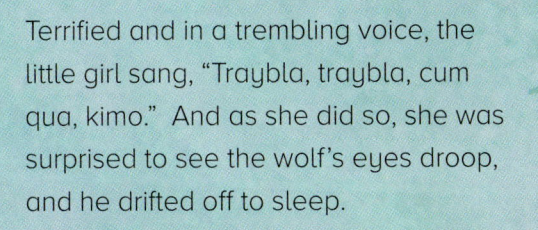

Terrified and in a trembling voice, the little girl sang, "Traybla, traybla, cum qua, kimo." And as she did so, she was surprised to see the wolf's eyes droop, and he drifted off to sleep.

The little girl took her chance and tiptoed across the meadow toward her house, but suddenly, she sneezed—ACHOO! And it woke up the wolf. He bounded toward the girl.

"Sing your sweet song to me again, little girl," he growled.

So, the frightened little girl sang again, "Traybla, traybla, cum qua, kimo." And once more, the wolf sank into a deep and pleasant slumber.

As quickly as she could, the little girl tiptoed toward her garden, but she stepped on a sharp stone—OUCH! And her cry woke up the snoozing wolf. He pounced toward her again.

"Sing your sweet song to me again," he growled, and he circled around her.

Plucking up all her courage, the little girl sang, "Traybla, traybla, cum qua, kimo." The wolf's eyelids soon grew heavy, and he slumped to the ground.

This time, the little girl tiptoed as carefully and quietly as she could, backing away from the sleeping wolf. When, at last, she reached her garden gate, she swung it open, dashed down her garden path, and the gate closed behind her with a loud SLAM!

The wolf jolted awake and sprinted toward her, but it was too late—she was safely behind her garden fence. He went home with an empty belly and a head full of lullaby, while the sweet little girl skipped inside with her sweet little bouquet, promising that she would always listen to her father from then on.

The Frog and the Condor

High in the mountains of Peru, the animals once had magical powers. The most powerful animal of all was the Condor, who could transform himself into a man.

One day, the Condor decided that he was tired of looking after his own nest, so he set out to look for a servant. He circled the mountains until he spotted a beautiful young shepherdess, who was herding llamas.

Perfect, thought the Condor, and as he landed, he shapeshifted into a man, wearing a smart black coat with a silky white scarf around his neck.

"Good day," said the Condor to the shepherdess. "What a healthy herd you have here. You must be good at your job." The shepherdess smiled and thanked him.

"What is your name?" he asked.

"Morning Star," said the shepherdess.

"You are certainly as beautiful as a star," said the Condor, and with each charming and flattering word, he inched slowly toward her.

When he reached her side, he quickly transformed into a bird again. Gripping the shepherdess in his talons, he flew away to his mountainside home, which was a large nest lined with llama fur, next to a dark cave filled with his supply of fresh meat.

The shepherdess was horrified and begged for her freedom, but the Condor was no longer charming—he was cruel and uncaring.

Morning Star was now his slave. Every day, the Condor hunted, ate, and slept, leaving her to clear out his nest, guard his pantry, and prepare his dinner. She was utterly miserable and often sat on the mountainside, looking sadly at the hills and dreaming of her home.

But Morning Star was not quite as alone as she thought. At the foot of the mountain, there burbled a cool, clear stream where a family of frogs liked to bathe. The eldest frog sister had a kind heart, but she believed herself to be very ugly.

When she saw her reflection in the stream, she often thought, *If only I could be as beautiful as my sisters.*

Every day, the frog sat and watched Morning Star and felt sorry for her. Sometimes, she croaked "Hello!", but the mountain was too high and the shepherdess couldn't hear her.

One morning, when the Condor had eaten his fill and was feeling content, Morning Star plucked up her courage to ask, "Please, sir, can I go down to the stream and wash my clothes? I have been wearing them for weeks."

The Condor was suspicious. "How do I know you won't try to escape?"

"You can see me from here!"

"But I want to rest," said the Condor.

"I promise to beat my clothes with rocks as I wash them. As long as you can hear the rocks, you know I am still there," said the shepherdess.

The Condor reluctantly agreed. "Very well, but I will hunt you down if you try to escape me."

Morning Star climbed down the mountain and was overjoyed to wash her face in the fresh, clean water of the stream. But as she began to wash her clothes, beating them with a rock, her eyes welled up with tears. If only she could escape the cruel Condor.

Suddenly, she heard a croaky voice. "Don't cry. I can help you."

Sitting on a rock before Morning Star was a little green frog.

"I wish you could, little frog. I am so unhappy," wept Morning Star.

"But I can," said the frog. "I don't have as much magic as the Condor, but I have enough to help you. I trust you are beating these rocks so that the Condor knows you are here?"

"Yes," said Morning Star.

"Well, I can take on your shape and beat the rocks for you. You'll have just enough time to run across the valley and escape, but you must be quick. There is a kind shepherd who lives over the hill. He will help you."

Morning Star could not believe her good fortune. Filled with hope, she leant forward and kissed the frog.

A moment later, it had taken on the shepherdess's shape and was beating the rocks, while Morning Star escaped across the valley.

An hour passed, and the old Condor was feeling hungry again.

What's taking the girl so long? he thought. He stretched his wings and peered down from his nest. He could see Morning Star still beating away at her clothes. He flew down to the stream and perched beside her.

"Enough of that!" he cried. "It's time for my dinner. Get back to the nest!"

But Morning Star stood up, and to the Condor's great surprise, she jumped into the shallow stream and disappeared!

The Condor could only see a little green frog, which he tried to peck at.

He was so angry, he let out a piercing shriek that echoed across the whole valley, and he flapped up and down looking for the shepherdess, but she had vanished. Enraged, he flew back to his mountain nest and never looked for a servant again.

Meanwhile, the little frog swam back upstream to her brothers and sisters. When they saw her, they all gasped and crowded around her.

"What's the matter?" she asked, worried that the Condor might have pulled off one of her legs.

"Sister!" they cried. "Look at your reflection!"

The little frog studied her reflection in the stream. She was amazed to see a shining star-shaped jewel on her forehead, exactly where Morning Star had kissed her. She looked beautiful!

Never again did the kind little frog think of herself as ugly.

The Tree of Dreams

Uaica was a young hunter in the Juruna tribe, and he lived in the heart of Brazil, at the edge of a tropical forest.

One day, Uaica was hunting for deer in the forest when he came across an ancient tree he had never seen before. The tree's branches reached far above the forest canopy. Its roots ran deep into the ground below.

Uaica wondered how he had never noticed the tree before, when he saw something quite peculiar. Around the trunk of the tree, a large group of animals lay sound asleep. There was a jaguar, a tapir, a spider monkey, a macaw, and a peccary, all curled up together.

Uaica approached the tree to take a closer look, and as he did so, he became overwhelmed by tiredness. Though he feared he was being bewitched, he could not keep his eyes open a moment longer. He yawned and stretched, and he lay down with the animals. Uaica fell asleep and drifted into a vivid dream.

In his dream, Sinaa came to him. Sinaa was a powerful god that was half-jaguar and half-man. Sinaa told Uaica tales about his ancestors and showed him strange animals he had never seen. Sinaa taught Uaica the secrets of the forest.

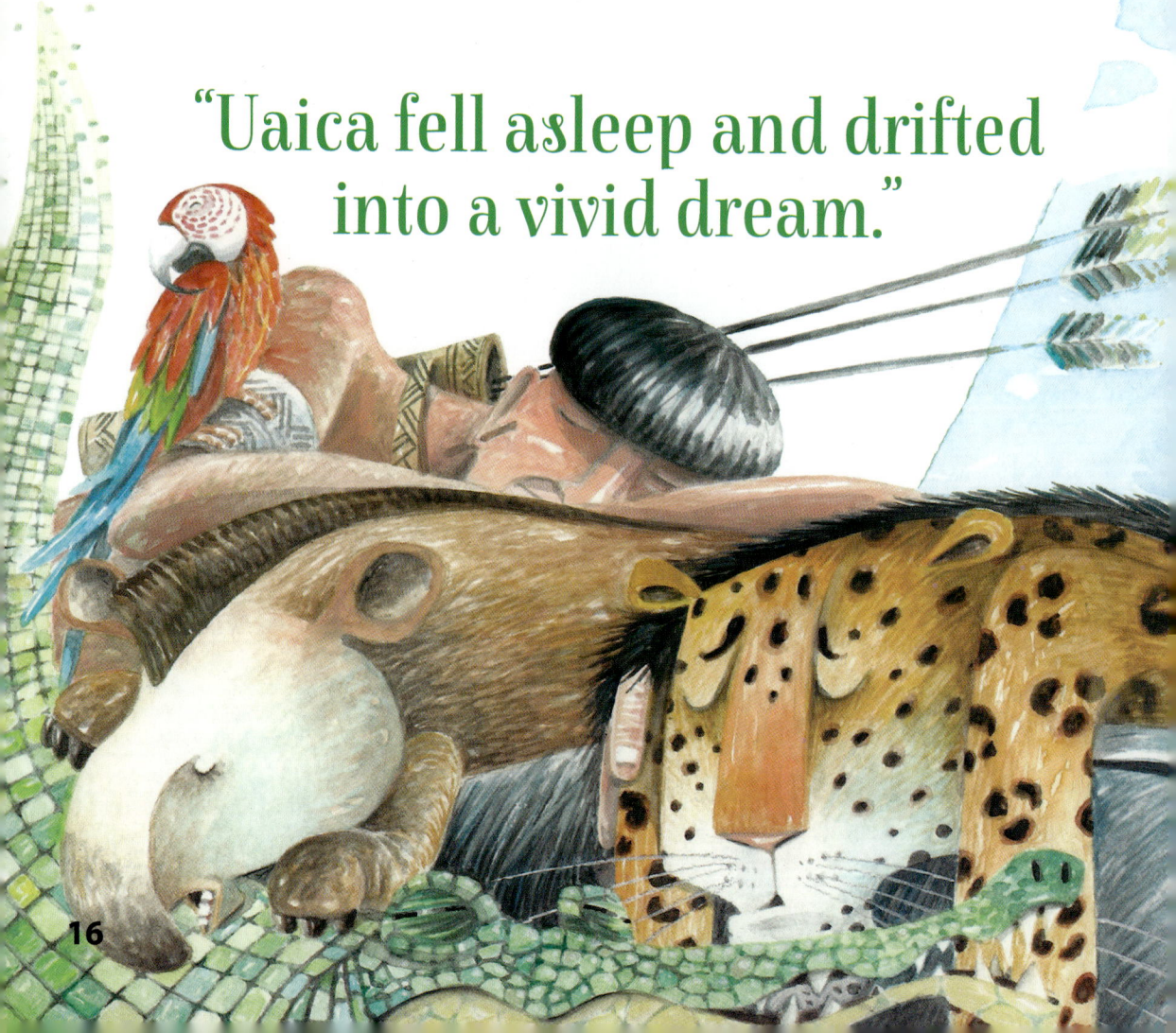

"Uaica fell asleep and drifted into a vivid dream."

When Uaica awoke from his mystical dream, he felt refreshed and happy, but all the animals had gone and it was dark, so Uaica ran home as quickly as he could. The other members of his tribe were angry that he had returned without food, but he didn't tell anyone of his strange experience.

The next day, Uaica returned to the tree of dreams, and the same thing happened again. Sinaa came to Uaica and shared more of his wisdom and magic. Uaica returned to the tree many times after that, and his tribe grew very angry with him for not hunting.

One day, Sinaa told him that his teachings were complete. He instructed Uaica to go home and share his new powers with his tribe. Sinaa gave Uaica some of the tree's bark to help his powers grow.

Uaica used the bark to make tea, and he drank some every day. He found that it gave him the magical power to heal. A few weeks passed, and a child became sick in his tribe—Uaica was able to cure her illness with the touch of his hand. It was a miracle, and the news of his amazing healing powers spread quickly.

Soon, many tribes throughout the forest came to visit Uaica, and he could cure anyone—even the animals. He drank the tree bark tea often, and over the years, his mystical dreams returned and he became a powerful medicine man.

The tribe wanted Uaica to marry and have children to carry on his powers. They begged him every day to choose a wife. Uaica didn't want to marry. But he grew tired of being pestered, so he married to please the tribe. His new wife soon grew jealous of the time Uaica spent helping other people. She nagged him so much that the tribe chased her away without Uaica's knowledge.

This angered the wife's family. So one night, the wife's brother crept up behind Uaica and tried to strike him over the head with a heavy club. Thanks to his magical powers, Uaica sensed that the brother was coming and ducked out of the way just in time. He was unharmed but upset that someone would try to harm him after all he had done to help his tribe.

That night, Uaica decided that he could not serve his tribe any longer. He left his village and walked deep into the forest. Some of the tribe members followed him to beg him to come back, but when they found him, he was sitting on a large rock in a dream-like trance. Nothing they could do would stir him.

By morning, Uaica was gone. He had disappeared into the dreamland of Sinaa, the Jaguar Man. With him, he took the secrets of healing and the wisdom of the forest—and because of their nagging, the tribe had lost its medicine man.

The Language of Birds

Long ago in Russia, there was a boy called Ivan, who was the son of a rich merchant. For all Ivan's good fortune, he longed with all his heart to understand the language of birds.

Ivan owned a caged nightingale, and every evening, after dinner, he would listen to the bird's sweet song and long to know what it meant.

One day, he went hunting in the forest, and the wind suddenly started to whip around him. The rain lashed down and the thunder rumbled. Ivan ran to shelter under a large tree and noticed a nest with four baby birds in its branches.

Worried about the chicks, he decided to climb the tree and drape his cloak over their nest to protect them.

Eventually, the thunderstorm passed, and the chicks' mother—a beautiful owl—returned to the nest. When she saw what Ivan had done, she spoke to him in a clear voice: "Thank you for protecting my children, kind sir. What can I give you in return?"

"I have a good life," said Ivan, "but there is one thing I wish for. Can you teach me the language of birds?"

The mother owl agreed. "Stay here with me for three days, and I will teach you all I can," she said.

Ivan stayed in the forest, and at the end of three days, he understood the language of birds. He set out for home, excited by his new gift.

That evening, after dinner with his parents, Ivan's nightingale began to sing, and he listened attentively. Soon, he started to weep.

"What is wrong, son?" asked his father.

"It's so terribly sad!" said Ivan, and tears rolled down his cheeks.

"What has happened?" demanded his father, who was starting to feel frightened by his son's crying.

"Oh, Father," explained Ivan, "when I was in the forest, I learnt the language of birds, and now I understand my nightingale's song. It is so sad."

"You are scaring us, Ivan! What did it sing?" cried his mother.

"The nightingale sang that one day, I will no longer be your son and you, Father, will be my servant."

"Nonsense!" said his father. However, that night, he couldn't sleep as he was so troubled by what Ivan had heard.

Over the following days, Ivan sat for hours listening to his nightingale, and slowly, his parents started to believe that he would betray them in some way and steal their fortune.

One night, when Ivan was sleeping soundly, his father carried him to the harbor, placed him in a rowing boat, and pushed him out to sea.

By the time Ivan awoke, he was far from land, and he spent a desperate night bobbing on the waves, until the sailors of a passing ship spotted his boat and helped him aboard.

Soon after Ivan boarded the ship, some birds flew overhead, and Ivan heard them talk of an approaching storm. He rushed to warn the ship's captain.

"Captain, the birds say there will be a terrible storm tonight. I think you should enter the nearest port."

The captain laughed at Ivan, and all the other sailors joined in—but that night, there came a storm that lashed and tore at the sails, tearing them to pieces. It took days to repair the ship.

A week later, Ivan saw some wild swans flying by, chatting noisily to each other. This time, the captain asked Ivan what they said.

"There is a notorious band of pirates close by," said Ivan. "They plan to rob any ships that pass. I think we should find a safe harbor."

This time, the crew listened to Ivan and made haste to the nearest port. From there, they saw the pirates attack many merchant ships.

The captain thanked Ivan and invited him to stay aboard. Ivan agreed, and they set off across the seas.

Before long, they dropped anchor in the main port of a country ruled by a wealthy king.

Word quickly reached the ship that the king was being plagued by three noisy crows who were constantly squawking by the window of his bedchamber and wouldn't go away.

The king was so desperate for a peaceful night's sleep that, on his orders, his guards had posted notices all over town, declaring that whoever could rid him of the crows would win his youngest daughter's hand in marriage. However, anyone who failed would have his head cut off!

Ivan hoped that his knowledge of the language of birds would bring him luck, and he headed for the palace. Once there, he was escorted to the king's bedroom, where he asked a servant to open the windows. The servants were quite puzzled to see Ivan sit down and do nothing. After a while, he asked the servants to take him to the king.

Ivan found the king seated on his throne, looking drained and tired. He bowed before him.

"Sire, I speak the language of birds, and the three crows at your window are mother, father, and son. They are arguing about whether the son should follow his mother or father in life. They want you to decide."

Wearily and with great doubt at Ivan's ability, the king yawned and said, "The son should follow his father."

Ivan conveyed the king's message to the crows, and immediately, they flew away, never to be seen again! The exhausted king was so overjoyed that, as well as marrying Ivan to the princess, he also gave him half his kingdom.

While all this had been happening, far away, Ivan's mother had died from old age, and his father felt so guilty at the way he had treated his son that he gave up work. He gradually lost his fortune and his home, and he was forced to travel from one town to the next, begging for food and shelter.

One day, his travels led him to the door of Ivan's palace, and when Ivan saw him, he knew immediately that it was his father. However, Ivan's father didn't recognize his son, as he was dressed in all his royal finery.

"What can I do for you, old man?" Ivan inquired.

"If you are good enough, sir, I would happily work as your faithful and humble servant in exchange for some food and shelter," said the old man.

"Oh, Father!" smiled Ivan. "Can't you recognize your own son? It seems that the nightingale's song turned out to be true, after all!"

Ivan's father then realised that he was looking at his son. Suddenly, all his grief vanished. He threw his arms around Ivan and begged for his forgiveness.

The old man did not become his son's servant, of course—Ivan's heart was far too kind. Instead, he forgave his father and made sure that he lived his last years in great comfort—and in the company of a caged nightingale.

Brer Rabbit

One sunny spring morning, Brer Fox decided to plant himself a vegetable patch. He found a lush corner of a field, and he dug, turned, and raked the soil until it looked rich and black.

When it was ready, he planted row after row of delicious peas. While Brer Fox was hard at work, Brer Rabbit had been peeking through the hedge, watching him. He dashed back to his children and, chuckling away, he sang to them:

"Ti-yi! Tungalee! I eat a pea, I pick a pea, It grows in the ground, it grows free! Ti-yi! Delicious peas!"

"Ti-yi! Tungalee! I eat a pea, I pick a pea. It grows in the ground, it grows free! Ti-yi! Delicious peas!"

And sure enough, when Brer Fox's peas had grown and ripened, every time he went to the field to harvest his patch, he found that somebody had already been there before him, stealing the fresh pea pods from the vines. He was furious!

But Brer Fox was also no fool—he had a good idea who the culprit was. He knew it must be Brer Rabbit—but he couldn't prove it because he always covered his tracks so well!

One afternoon, when Brer Fox had really had enough of the pea thief, he walked up and down the field, looking for a little gap in the hedge where he was sure Brer Rabbit was squeezing through. When he found the rabbit-sized gap, he gathered some ropes and laid a trap.

"Ti-yi! Tungalee!"

The next morning, when Brer Rabbit came sneaking along, he bounded through the hedge as usual—and Brer Fox's trap sprang straight into action.

A loop of rope knotted itself around Brer Rabbit's back legs, and he was flung into the air, where he was left swinging from the top of a small tree. As he dangled there, Brer Rabbit wasn't sure whether to be scared of falling down or scared of getting stuck there—and what he was most afraid of was what Brer Fox would do to him when he found him.

As he tried to come up with a clever excuse, he heard heavy footsteps lumbering down the road.

Soon, Brer Bear appeared, ambling along, with his paws covered in honey from a morning of bothering beehives.

Brer Rabbit called out, "Hey! Hello there, Brer Bear!"

Brer Bear was a little surprised to see Brer Rabbit dangling from a tree.

"Umm...Hello, Brer Rabbit! How are you doing on this fine morning?"

"Thanks for asking, Brer Bear. I'm doing pretty well," said Brer Rabbit.

"What are you doing up there in the heavens, Brer Rabbit?" asked Brer Bear.

"Brer Fox is paying me a dollar a minute to guard his pea patch from the birds," said Brer Rabbit. "In fact, he said if Brer Bear comes along, I should ask him if he wants to do it instead, as he has a big family to care for and would be even better at scaring away the pesky birds."

Wow! A dollar a minute! thought Brer Bear.

"That sounds like easy money to me!" And he jumped at Brer Rabbit's sneaky job offer.

Brer Rabbit asked his bear friend to untie the knot around his back legs, and made his escape from the trap. In just a few minutes, poor Brer Bear was swinging from the top of the tree in Brer Rabbit's place.

Brer Rabbit waved goodbye to Brer Bear, then he hopped all the way over to Brer Fox's place as quickly as he could and cried out, "Brer Fox! Brer Fox! Come right away and see the thief who's been stealing from your pea patch!"

Brer Fox dashed out of his house and ran up the lane with Brer Rabbit.

"There he is!" said Brer Rabbit, pointing at Brer Bear, who was still hanging from the tree, licking honey from his paws.

"Got you, pea thief!" cried Brer Fox, and before Brer Bear could explain how he had been tricked, Brer Fox started to holler at him, scolding him for stealing his peas.

In the middle of all this hullabaloo, Brer Rabbit slipped away to find the best hiding place he could, because he knew Brer Bear would be so mad at him for tricking him, he'd come looking for him when he was freed.

So, Brer Rabbit slipped into a muddy pond and stayed there, with only his two eyes poking out. A little while later, Brer Bear came stomping down the lane in a bad mood.

"Good day, Brer Frog," he growled. "Have you seen Brer Rabbit about?"

"Yes, indeed," croaked Brer Rabbit. "He went hopping by that-a-way a short time ago. Ribbit!"

Brer Bear ran off down the lane at great speed, and cheeky Brer Rabbit climbed out of the pond. He shook himself off and, with a grin on his face, headed for home with a secret stash of peas in his pocket.

31

Book Club Questions

1. How can traditional stories help you learn more about cultures around the world?

2. Compare and contrast "The Frog and the Condor" and "The Tree of Dreams."

3. Many of these stories contain animals that are unique to the area from which the story came. What animals might be in a story from your hometown?

4. How are the girl in "Wolf Lullaby" and the boy in "The Language of Birds" similar?

5. Would you rather have Uaica's power to heal or Ivan's power to understand birds? Explain your answer.

6. How would you rewrite the ending of "Brer Rabbit" if you had the chance?